W9-CNP-949

A NOTE TO PARENTS

When your children are ready to "step into reading," giving them the right books is as crucial as giving them the right food to eat. **Step into Reading Books** present exciting stories and information reinforced with lively, colorful illustrations that make learning to read fun, satisfying, and worthwhile. They are priced so that acquiring an entire library of them is affordable. And they are beginning readers with a difference—they're written on five levels.

Early Step into Reading Books are designed for brand-new readers, with large type and only one or two lines of very simple text per page. **Step 1 Books** feature the same easy-to-read type as the Early Step into Reading Books, but with more words per page. **Step 2 Books** are both longer and slightly more difficult, while **Step 3 Books** introduce readers to paragraphs and fully developed plot lines. **Step 4 Books** offer exciting nonfiction for the increasingly independent reader.

Copyright © 1998 Children's Television Workshop (CTW).
Jim Henson's Sesame Street Muppets copyright © 1998 The Jim Henson Company.
Sesame Street and the Sesame Street sign are trademarks and service marks of Children's
Television Workshop. All rights reserved under International and Pan-American Copyright
Conventions. Published in the United States of America and simultaneously in Canada by
CTW Publishing Company L.L.C., a joint venture of Children's Television Workshop and
Random House, Inc. Distributed by Random House, Inc.

www.randomhouse.com/kids/
www.sesamestreet.com

Library of Congress Cataloging-in-Publication Data
Hayward, Linda.
Baker, baker, cookie maker / by Linda Hayward ; illustrated by Tom Brannon.
    p. cm. — (Step into reading. A step 1 book) "Featuring Jim Henson's Sesame Street Muppets."
SUMMARY: Cookie Monster bakes beautiful and tempting cookies in his bakery,
but he has so many customers that he cannot even have a taste.
ISBN 0-679-88379-7 (pbk.) — ISBN 0-679-98379-1 (lib. bdg.) [1. Cookies—Fiction.
2. Baking—Fiction. 3. Puppets—Fiction. 4. Stories in rhyme.] I. Brannon, Tom, ill.
II. Title. III. Series: Step into reading. Step 1 book.
PZ8.3.C625Bak 1998 [E]—dc21 97-34641

Printed in the United States of America 10 9 8 7 6 5 4 3 2 1

STEP INTO READING is a registered trademark of Random House, Inc.

Step into Reading®

Baker, Baker, Cookie Maker

Featuring
Jim Henson's
Sesame Street
Muppets

By Linda Hayward
Illustrated by Tom Brannon

A Step 1 Book

CTW Publishing

Cookie Monster,
cookie eater,
mixes batter
with his beater,

drops the dough
onto the sheet,

bakes the cookies.
Good to eat!

He puts the cookies
on a plate,
takes a cookie...
Oops, too late!

Baker, baker,
cookie maker,
here comes a hungry
cookie taker!

COOKIES! COOKIES!

Monster treat.

Some for munchers,
some for crunchers,

none for the baker
on Sesame Street.

Cookie Monster,
cookie cutter,
makes a batch
with peanut butter,

cuts the cookies
out of dough,

puts them on the plate...
Oh, no!

Baker, baker,
cookie maker,
here comes another
cookie taker!

COOKIES! COOKIES!

Monster treat.

Some for hikers,
some for bikers,

none for the baker

on Sesame Street.

Cookie Monster,
cookie master,
makes more cookies
even faster.

He pats the cookies
nice and flat;
makes them,
bakes them.
Look at that!

Baker, baker,
cookie maker,
here come some *more*
cookie takers!

COOKIES! COOKIES!

Monster treat.

Some for hoppers,
some for moppers,

and *one* for the baker

on Sesame Street.